A MODERN FRONT WH[...]

D1144631

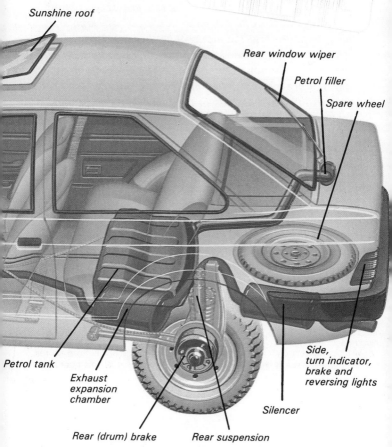

Sunshine roof

Rear window wiper

Petrol filler

Spare wheel

Petrol tank

Exhaust expansion chamber

Rear (drum) brake

Rear suspension

Silencer

Side, turn indicator, brake and reversing lights

The motor car as we now know it has developed from its early beginnings in the 1870s when it began to replace the horse drawn carriage which was the main means of land transport in those days. The modern car has many similarities to the old 'horseless carriages' of Daimler, Benz, Panhard and the numerous other inventors of that age, but engineers now know much more about how and why things work and can use their knowledge to design cars that are more efficient and more comfortable. They also have better materials to use which are lighter and stronger and computers to help them to make the best use of these advantages. In addition modern machinery enables these complicated vehicles to be made in large numbers economically.

The present day car is a complex piece of machinery involving advanced technology. The basic principles of how it works however are not difficult to understand and it is hoped that this book with the aid of its clear illustrations and diagrams will help.

Acknowledgment:
The publishers gratefully acknowledge the assistance of the Ford Motor Company and Lucas Electrical Ltd in the preparation of this book.

Revised edition

Published by Ladybird Books Ltd Loughborough Leicestershire UK
Ladybird Books Inc Lewiston Maine 04240 USA

HOW IT WORKS...
THE MOTOR CAR

by ALAN W WILDIG BSc(Eng), CEng, MIMechE
Loughborough University of Technology

with illustrations by
GERALD WITCOMB MSIAD

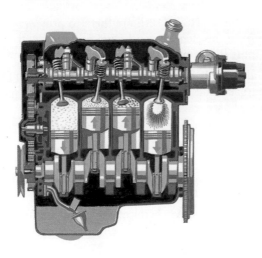

Ladybird Books

The motor car

The function of a motor car is to provide transport for people. To do this it needs an ENGINE to develop the power to drive it and a GEARBOX and FINAL DRIVE (together known as the TRANSMISSION) to transmit the power to the driving wheels, which may be either at the front or at the rear of the vehicle. For the driver to be able to control the car he needs a BRAKING SYSTEM to slow it down and stop it and a STEERING SYSTEM to guide the car in the correct direction.

For the comfort of the driver and passengers there are FRONT AND REAR SUSPENSIONS to smooth out the bumps whilst at the same time keeping the wheels in contact with the road.

The BODY AND STRUCTURE are there to provide protection from the elements and from accidents and also to support the component parts.

The car also needs an ELECTRICAL SYSTEM to enable the engine to run and to supply power for the lights and instruments.

These units are depicted in the drawing of a modern car inside the front cover whilst its engine is shown on the opposite page. In this book the engine will be described first and then we will go on to look at all the other components in the order outlined above.

The engine converts the chemical energy of the fuel into the mechanical energy necessary to power the vehicle. Its major components are shown in the diagram. It is recommended that as you read in the following pages about the various items that go to make the engine and the rest of the vehicle you refer back to these diagrams to see how they fit into the complete assembly.

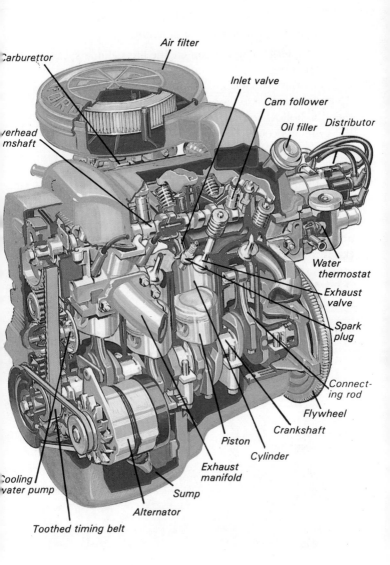

Carburettor

Air filter

Inlet valve

Cam follower

Oil filler

Distributor

Overhead camshaft

Water thermostat

Exhaust valve

Spark plug

Connecting rod

Flywheel

Crankshaft

Piston

Cylinder

Exhaust manifold

Sump

Alternator

Cooling water pump

Toothed timing belt

The engine — pistons and crankshaft

Every internal combustion engine has cylinders; these are really holes which are bored accurately down the depth of the cylinder block so that the pistons can move up and down inside them. Around the cylinders the metal is hollow so that water can be circulated to keep the cylinders cool.

Power is developed by burning a petrol and air mixture in the cylinders which are sealed at the top by the cylinder head. The burning mixture expands and pushes the piston downwards.

The connecting rods link the pistons to the crankshaft and this enables the up and down motion of the piston (known as the 'stroke') to be translated into the rotary motion of the crankshaft, as shown in the diagram; the crankshaft can then drive the wheels via the transmission.

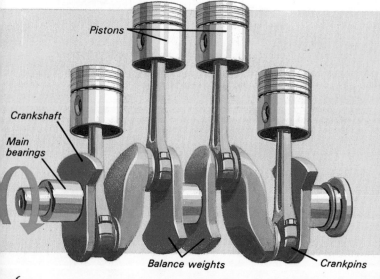

Pistons

Crankshaft

Main bearings

Balance weights

Crankpins

The diagrams on pages 6 and 7 show the names of the various parts of the assembly.

The piston rings fit around the pistons and press against the cylinder walls to prevent gases escaping downward past the piston whilst at the same time allowing only the minimum amount of oil necessary to lubricate the cylinder, to pass upwards from the sump.

The shell bearings at the crankshaft end are used to reduce the friction between the big ends and the crankshaft; they consist of a strong steel outer shell with soft bearing-metal inside and this runs on the crankpin.

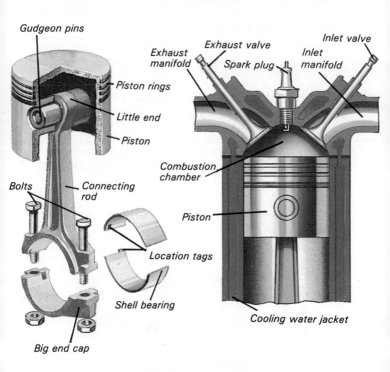

Gudgeon pins

Exhaust manifold

Exhaust valve

Spark plug

Inlet valve

Inlet manifold

Piston rings

Little end

Piston

Combustion chamber

Bolts

Connecting rod

Piston

Location tags

Shell bearing

Big end cap

Cooling water jacket

The four-stroke cycle

Practically all car engines operate on the four-stroke cycle. This means that the piston travels up and down twice between each ignition of the petrol/air mixture. The cycle of operations shown in the diagram is as follows:

1 **Induction:** The inlet valve opens and as the piston moves downwards a petrol/air mixture is drawn past the valve, into the cylinder.

2 **Compression:** As the piston completes the previous downstroke the inlet valve closes. The rotating crankshaft pushes the piston upwards, compressing the mixture in the cylinder into the combustion chamber at the top.

3 **Power:** At the piston's highest point (called *top dead centre*) a spark jumps across the electrodes of the spark plug. This ignites the petrol/air mixture; the resulting heat causes the burning mixture to expand which pushes the piston down.

4 **Exhaust:** Towards the end of the downstroke the exhaust valve opens and on the following upstroke the waste products of combustion are pushed past the exhaust valve and out of the engine. The exhaust valve then closes and this is followed by the induction stroke of the next cycle and so on.

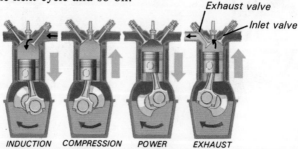

INDUCTION   COMPRESSION   POWER   EXHAUST

These cycles will be repeated about 28 times every second in a car travelling at 96 km/h (60 mph).

The four-cylinder four-stroke engine

Most cars have either four- or six-cylinder engines although there are some with as many as twelve cylinders; their size and number depend upon the power required. The crankshaft shown on page 6 has two pistons that are up (said to be at *top dead centre*) and two that are down (*bottom dead centre*). This arrangement helps to balance the engine and also ensures that the firing strokes are at equal intervals.

The figure below shows a modern four-cylinder engine. Since it is working on the four-stroke cycle each cylinder will be on a different stroke. We number the cylinders from the front and the usual firing order is 1–3–4–2; thus if No. 1 piston is on the induction stroke then No. 2 will be on compression, No. 4 firing and No. 3 on the exhaust stroke.

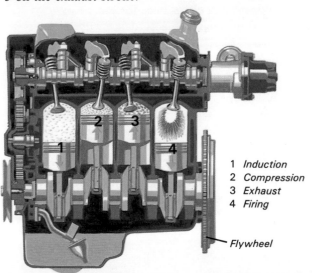

1 *Induction*
2 *Compression*
3 *Exhaust*
4 *Firing*

Flywheel

A heavy wheel is attached to the rear of the crankshaft; this is called the *flywheel* and its purpose is to smooth out the power from the cylinders. It also helps to turn the crankshaft past the 'dead centre' position of the pistons and provides a very convenient place to mount the clutch.

The more cylinders an engine has, the smoother running it will be and the smaller the flywheel it will need.

The valves and camshaft

Each cylinder has an inlet and exhaust valve and these must open and close at the correct instant in the engine cycle. The valves are operated through 'followers' or 'tappets'. These move up and down in guides and are lifted by means of 'cams' which are specially shaped lobes of metal and are made as part of the camshaft.

The camshaft is driven by means of a chain or a toothed belt at half the speed of the crankshaft so that each valve opens and closes once for every two revolutions of the engine in accordance with the four-stroke cycle.

Note that the cam *lifts* the valve but it is returned on to its seat in the cylinder head by the valve spring which is fitted around the valve stem.

All car engines now have the inlet and exhaust valves above the pistons and are known as overhead valve engines.

In the engine illustrated on the right the tappets operate the valves through a system of rods and levers, but in the most recent engines the camshafts are over the cylinders and then the cams operate the valves directly; this means that the engine can rotate at higher speeds.

The engine illustrated on the right below has two overhead camshafts (twin OHC) one for the inlet valves and one for the exhaust. This would be for a high performance car but it is more usual to have a single overhead camshaft (single OHC) as shown on page 5.

◁ LOW CAMSHAFT

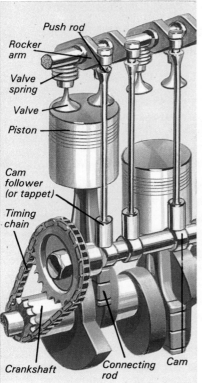

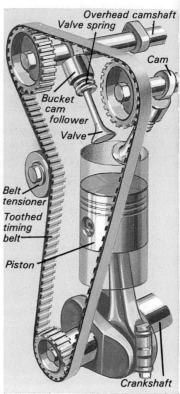

TWIN OVERHEAD CAMSHAFT ▷

The ignition system

For the four-stroke cycle to work it is necessary for the petrol/air mixture in the cylinders to be ignited precisely as the pistons reach top dead centre on the compression stroke. To achieve this a spark must jump across the electrodes of the spark plugs and a very high voltage (electrical pressure) must be supplied to them.

To step up the voltage from the 12V available from the battery to the 25000V necessary to cause the spark to jump, a *coil* is used.

The coil consists in fact of two coils of wire wound one on top of the other over an iron core. The outer coil, known as the primary winding, consists of about 300 complete turns of comparatively thick wire, whilst the inner coil, the secondary winding, has some 20,000 turns of very fine wire.

When a current is passed through the primary circuit (shown in orange in the diagram) and then the circuit is suddenly broken, it produces a very high voltage in the secondary winding (shown red). This voltage is conveyed to the *rotor arm* via the *distributor* which sends it to whichever cylinder is about to fire.

The primary circuit current passes to earth through the *contact breaker* points in the distributor. When the cam at the top of the distributor drive shaft causes these points to separate, the primary circuit is broken and the spark jumps across the electrodes of the spark plug in the firing cylinder. There are the same number of lobes on the cam as there are cylinders in the engine.

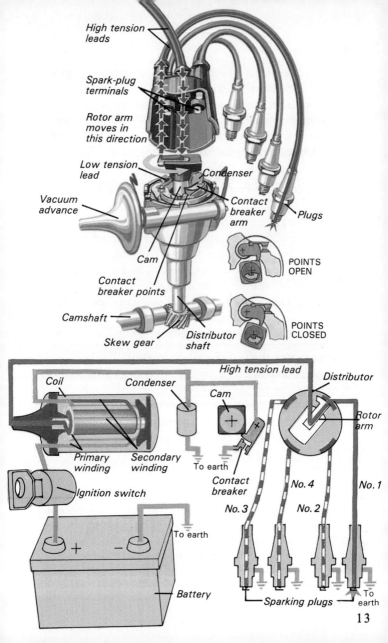

High tension leads

Spark-plug terminals

Rotor arm moves in this direction

Low tension lead

Vacuum advance

Condenser

Contact breaker arm

Plugs

Cam

Contact breaker points

POINTS OPEN

Camshaft

Skew gear

Distributor shaft

POINTS CLOSED

High tension lead

Coil

Condenser

Cam

Distributor

Rotor arm

Primary winding

Secondary winding

To earth

Contact breaker

No. 4

No. 1

Ignition switch

No. 3

No. 2

To earth

Battery

Sparking plugs

To earth

13

The fuel system

A mixture of petrol and air is burnt in the engine to provide the energy to drive the car. The petrol has to be stored in the *fuel tank* and supplied to the engine via the *carburettor* as required. Petrol is highly inflammable and its vapour when mixed with air in a confined space can be explosive. The petrol tank therefore is located away from the engine. It is also positioned so that it will not burst in the event of an accident when sparks could start a serious fire.

With the engine at one end of the car and the fuel tank at the other, a pump is necessary to send the fuel from the tank to the carburettor. The diagram opposite shows two views of the *fuel pump*. The pump is driven by the engine, usually from an additional cam on the camshaft. The operating rod moves up and down and works a diaphragm which is held at its circumference and moved by the rod at its centre.

Thus, when the rod moves downwards (a) the diaphragm moves down and petrol is drawn through the one-way valve on the right. When the rod moves upwards the one-way valve closes and the fuel above the diaphragm is pushed out to the engine through the one-way valve on the left (b). Then the one-way valve on the left closes so that the fuel cannot be sucked back from the engine whilst the valve on the right opens allowing more fuel to be taken from the tank.

The fuel tank holds enough petrol for about 500 km (310 miles) running, (about 55 litres (12 gallons) for a medium size car.) A sensor in the tank sends a signal to the fuel gauge on the dashboard to tell the driver how much fuel there is left in the tank.

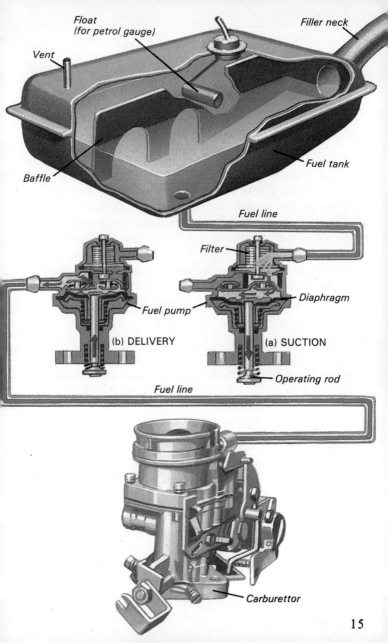

Float
(for petrol gauge)

Filler neck

Vent

Baffle

Fuel tank

Fuel line

Filter

Fuel pump

(b) DELIVERY

Diaphragm

(a) SUCTION

Operating rod

Fuel line

Carburettor

15

The carburettor

The function of the carburettor is to mix air with petrol from the fuel system in the correct proportion (about 15 parts of air to 1 of petrol by weight) and then to pass the mixture to the engine for burning in the cylinders.

The diagram on the right shows the principle on which carburettors work but in practice they are rather more complicated. Petrol is supplied to the float chamber from the fuel system and the needle valve shuts off the flow when the correct level is reached. Air is drawn via an air cleaner or filter through the choke tube by the pistons of the engine when they are on their induction strokes; it is made to pass through a reduced area known as the *venturi* at the point where the tube from the float chamber protrudes into the choke tube.

This has the effect of reducing the pressure there, so that the atmospheric pressure within the float chamber can push the petrol out into the choke tube. On its way it has to pass through the main jet which restricts the flow; at the end of the tube where it emerges there are a number of radial drillings that cause the petrol to form a uniform mist in the airstream as it enters the cylinders.

The flow of combustible mixture and hence the speed and power output of the engine is controlled by the *throttle butterfly* which is opened when the driver presses the *accelerator*.

When the engine is being started from cold, a richer mixture is required. To achieve this the choke flap is partially closed either by the driver or automatically. This restricts the flow of air and increases the suction on the petrol passing through the main jet.

Many high performance and racing cars use petrol injection instead of a carburettor. A throttle butterfly operated by the accelerator pedal regulates the amount of air passing into the cylinder whilst a pump pressurises the petrol which is then squirted directly into the cylinders through injectors. The timing and the quantity of petrol injected can be precisely controlled by electronic means.

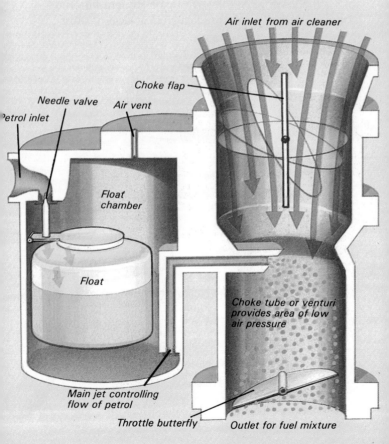

Air inlet from air cleaner

Choke flap

Needle valve

Air vent

Petrol inlet

Float chamber

Float

Choke tube or venturi provides area of low air pressure

Main jet controlling flow of petrol

Throttle butterfly

Outlet for fuel mixture

The exhaust system

After combustion, the waste gases flow through the exhaust valve into the exhaust port and thence into the exhaust system, as shown in the diagram.

When these gases emerge into the exhaust port they are very hot and at a high pressure. The surge of gas, each time an exhaust valve opens, sets up shock waves, and if the gases were allowed to pass straight into the atmosphere they would produce a great deal of noise.

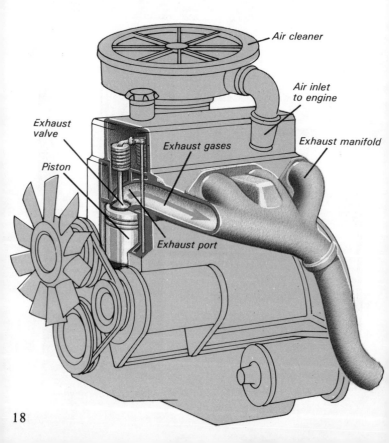

Air cleaner

Air inlet to engine

Exhaust valve

Exhaust gases

Piston

Exhaust manifold

Exhaust port

To prevent this the gases are passed down a length of exhaust pipe, cooling on the way, and then into a silencer. In its most common form the silencer is a metal box containing a series of baffles so that the gases have to follow a zig-zag path. In so doing they emerge from the tail pipe at a much reduced speed and produce less noise.

The exhaust manifold is a series of pipes that collect the exhaust gases from each cylinder and bring them together before passing them into the exhaust pipe. The manifold is carefully designed so that the maximum amount of exhaust gas is removed from each cylinder. This leaves more room for the incoming mixture and makes the engine more efficient.

Exhaust gas contains *carbon monoxide* which is poisonous and *carbon dioxide*. It also contains hydrocarbons from incompletely burnt fuel and oxides of nitrogen which are produced by the high temperatures in the cylinders; these in the atmosphere can cause smog and are particularly harmful to people suffering from respiratory diseases.

In addition, exhaust gas contains lead, another poison, which is added to fuel to improve the combustion process. Most countries have laws controlling the quantity of these pollutants allowed in vehicle emissions.

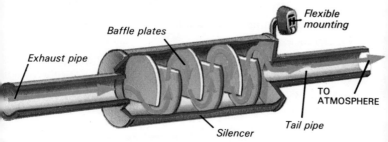

Flexible mounting

Baffle plates

Exhaust pipe

TO ATMOSPHERE

Silencer

Tail pipe

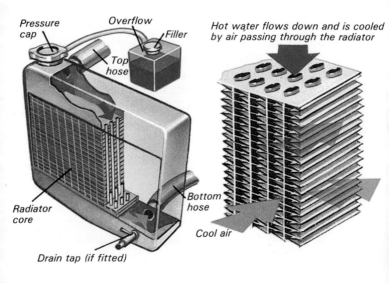

Pressure cap

Overflow

Filler

Top hose

Hot water flows down and is cooled by air passing through the radiator

Radiator core

Bottom hose

Cool air

Drain tap (if fitted)

The cooling system

Nearly all cars use water to bring the heat from the engine to the radiator where it is cooled. The water flows through spaces known as the *water jacket*, around the cylinders and valves and out of the top of the engine and thence to the top of the radiator. Cooling air, passing through the spaces in the radiator, takes away the heat from the water before it returns to the engine. The water is circulated by a water pump (or impeller) that is driven by a belt from the crankshaft. Many modern radiators are shallow but wide and have the water tubes running horizontally. These are known as *crossflow* radiators.

The water *thermostat* is a form of valve which causes the water to be re-circulated through the engine until it has reached its running temperature. This helps rapid warming up of the engine and car heater. Also incorporated either in the filler cap or in a special

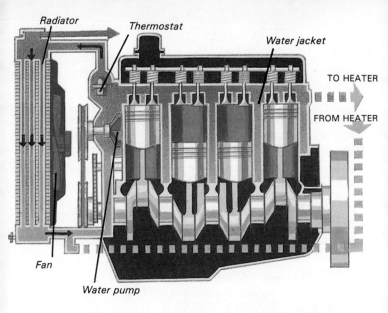

Radiator Thermostat Water jacket

TO HEATER

FROM HEATER

Fan

Water pump

pressure cap is a spring-loaded valve that discourages the water from boiling by pressurising the system.

Under most driving conditions there is sufficient cooling air flowing through the radiator. However, when the car is stationary in a traffic queue or working hard climbing a steep hill slowly, the air flow needs boosting. For this, most modern cars have cooling fans which are switched on by a thermostat.

When water freezes it expands and this can cause serious damage. To prevent this the water is mixed with 'anti-freeze' in winter.

The overflow from the radiator cap is led into the bottom of an overflow bottle. When the coolant expands it flows past the pressure cap into the bottle; as it cools down, coolant is drawn back. The bottle is usually translucent so that the level can be inspected without removing the filler cap.

Engine lubrication

In an engine there are many moving parts, some sliding and others rotating. No matter how smooth a metal surface may seem, it will be found to have 'mountains' and 'valleys'. These irregularities create resistance, known as friction. To reduce this friction, special bearing materials are placed between moving parts. The use of oil as a lubricant serves to keep these moving surfaces apart and to reduce the friction further.

When the engine is running, oil is pumped under pressure from a reservoir called the sump through various passages (or galleries) in the cylinder block and head to the moving parts.

The oil pump is driven either by a 'skew' gear from the camshaft (shown opposite) or directly off the crankshaft in the case of overhead camshaft engines. It draws its oil through a gauze filter submerged in the sump and this traps any coarse particles. The pressurised oil from the pump is delivered to the moving parts through a much finer filter and past a pressure limiting valve.

It is important that there is the correct quantity of oil in the sump. In order to check this every engine has a 'dip-stick' as shown.

Oil has other things to do besides reducing friction. It has to carry away excess heat from the bearing surfaces; it has to prevent corrosion and be able to absorb waste products of combustion that get past the pistons. In addition, the oil must not foam nor be too thick when cold nor too thin when hot.

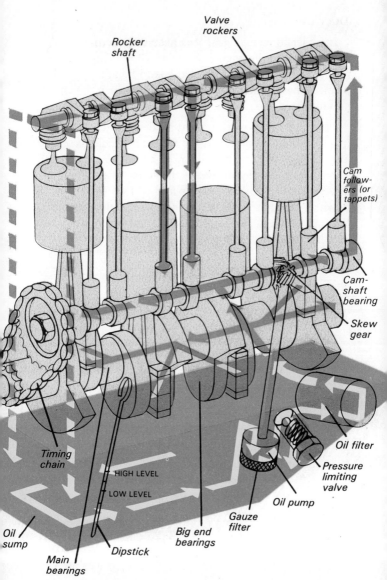

Valve rockers

Rocker shaft

Cam followers (or tappets)

Camshaft bearing

Skew gear

Timing chain

HIGH LEVEL

LOW LEVEL

Oil filter

Pressure limiting valve

Oil pump

Oil sump

Main bearings

Dipstick

Big end bearings

Gauze filter

23

The clutch

In order to change gear it is necessary to disconnect the drive from the engine to the gearbox. This is done by means of the clutch which also has to be able to reconnect the engine smoothly, especially when the car is moving from rest.

The diagram shows a typical modern clutch. The drive from the engine comes via the flywheel which, as we have already seen, is bolted to the end of the crankshaft. The clutch plate, by means of the spline at its centre, drives the shaft to the gearbox and is itself driven by the flywheel through the friction linings. The clutch plate is clamped between the pressure plate and the flywheel and the clamping force is applied through the powerful

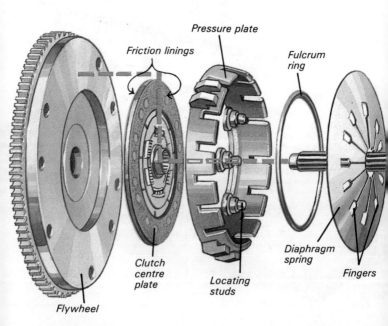

Pressure plate

Friction linings

Fulcrum ring

Clutch centre plate

Locating studs

Diaphragm spring

Fingers

Flywheel

diaphragm spring. This spring is initially conical but when it is assembled in the clutch it is flattened, and in trying to regain its original conical shape it exerts a strong clamping force on the pressure plate.

When the driver wishes to disengage the clutch he pushes on the clutch pedal which, through a system of levers, moves the release bearing to the left; this takes the load off the pressure plate and moves it away from the clutch plate. The clutch plate is then free and will not be driven by the engine.

To re-connect the drive, the driver releases the clutch pedal and the rate of re-engagement depends upon the speed with which he moves his foot.

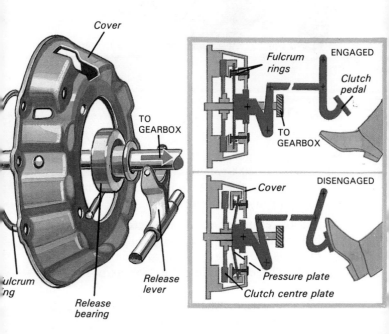

Cover

Fulcrum rings

ENGAGED

Clutch pedal

TO GEARBOX

TO GEARBOX

Cover

DISENGAGED

Fulcrum ring

Release lever

Release bearing

Pressure plate

Clutch centre plate

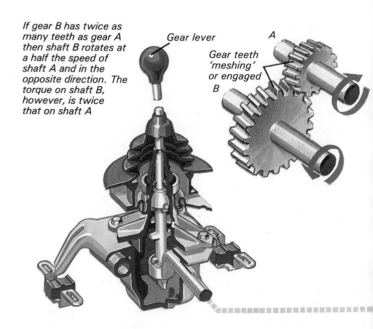

If gear B has twice as many teeth as gear A then shaft B rotates at a half the speed of shaft A and in the opposite direction. The torque on shaft B, however, is twice that on shaft A

Gear lever

A

Gear teeth 'meshing' or engaged

B

The gearbox

A typical car engine will run at rotational speeds from about 600 rpm to 6000 rpm but it will only produce the high power needed for acceleration or hill-climbing over the top part of this speed range.

A car is therefore equipped with a gearbox to enable the driver to alter the ratio of the speed of rotation of the engine relative to the speed of rotation of the roadwheels. This enables the higher powers, which the engine is capable of developing, to be available over the whole range of vehicle speed.

The engine always runs at faster speeds than the roadwheels: in high gear it will rotate about four times faster, whilst in bottom gear it will run at as much as fifteen times faster. The reduction in speed occurs partly in the gearbox and partly in the final drive by the use of gears 'meshing' as shown in the figure opposite.

The ratio of the speed of the input shaft to that of the output shaft is known as the 'gearbox ratio' and depends upon the numbers of teeth in the meshing gears. The gearbox of a front wheel drive vehicle usually has two shafts carrying as many pairs of gears as there are gear ratios.

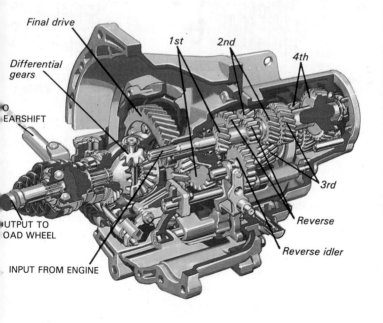

TRANSMISSION FOR FRONT WHEEL DRIVE CAR

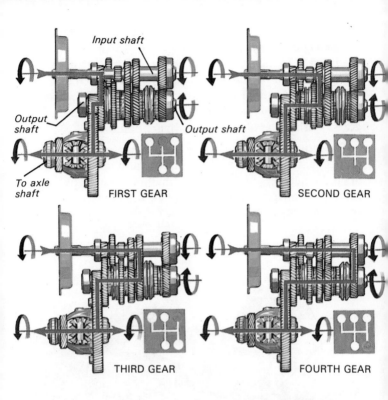

The gears are in constant mesh and run at different speeds according to the numbers of teeth. However, the gears on the output shaft run freely on it and only drive it when the appropriate gear is locked to it by the driver operating the gear lever. The power flow in the different gears is shown in the series of diagrams.

The ratio of the rotational speed of the gearbox output shaft to that of the axle shafts is known as the 'final drive ratio' and multiplying this by the gearbox ratio gives the 'overall gear ratio' of the transmission, that is, the ratio of the speed of the engine to that of the roadwheels.

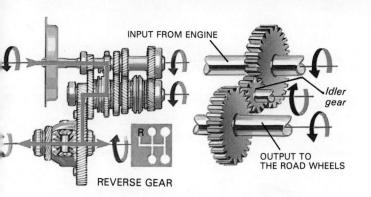

INPUT FROM ENGINE

Idler gear

OUTPUT TO THE ROAD WHEELS

R

REVERSE GEAR

To obtain reverse gear, an 'idler' gear is slid into mesh between two gears on the input and output shafts; this has the effect of reversing the direction of rotation of the output shaft and hence of the roadwheels themselves.

Gearboxes for cars having engines at the front driving the rear wheels have three shafts. In top gear the input shaft is connected to the output shaft (mainshaft) and drives it directly; in the other gears the 'layshaft' which is driven by the input shaft through gears A-B in turn drives the output shaft through gears C-D, E-F or G-H.

REAR WHEEL DRIVE GEARBOX

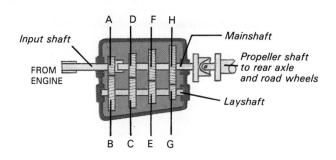

A   D   F   H

Input shaft

Mainshaft

Propeller shaft to rear axle and road wheels

FROM ENGINE

Layshaft

B   C   E   G

Front and rear wheel drives

At one time nearly all cars had the engine and gearbox at the front driving the rear wheels. However, the very successful BMC Mini showed that an arrangement with the engine mounted across the car (transverse) driving the front wheels gave the maximum space available in the vehicle for passengers and luggage. Nowadays most small and even medium size cars have adopted this layout.

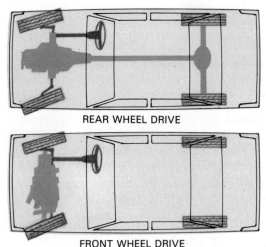

REAR WHEEL DRIVE

FRONT WHEEL DRIVE

Having the front wheels 'pulling' tends to make front wheel drive (FWD) cars handle better, especially under slippery conditions. Driving the front wheels however presents problems when turning and special constant velocity joints have to be fitted to the drive shafts to prevent the car cornering in a series of jerks. The rear wheel drive (RWD) car does not have this problem but instead has noise and vibration problems and a 'transmission tunnel' inside the car.

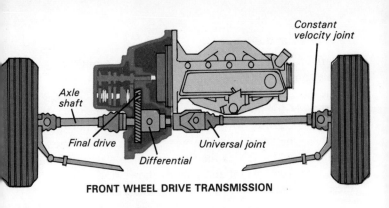

FRONT WHEEL DRIVE TRANSMISSION

When a vehicle accelerates, load comes off the front wheels and on to the rear ones. This helps the rear wheel drive (RWD) car but the front wheels of a FWD car are liable to spin. Similarly during braking, the load increases on the front wheels and decreases on the rear ones. FWD vehicles tend to have more of their weight on the front and so the braking system has to be designed to prevent the rear wheels from sliding during heavy braking.

Because of wheel spin problems and difficulty in accommodating large transverse engines between steered front wheels, powerful cars are still usually RWD.

Some special vehicles such as the Land and Range Rovers can drive all four wheels so that they can grip under slippery or heavy going conditions.

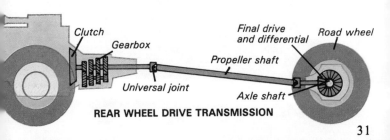

REAR WHEEL DRIVE TRANSMISSION

Final drive and differential

Part of the reduction in rotational speed from the engine to the roadwheels takes place in the final drive. In the case of the transmission shown on page 27 and top page 31 for the FWD car with a transverse engine, the final drive consists of two normal helical gears, but for a RWD car the drive from the propshaft has to be turned through 90°. To do this the final drive has a pair of bevel gears, the crown wheel and pinion, shown in the diagram; these are tapered gears that run together like two cones.

When a car goes round a corner, the outside wheel has to travel further, and hence faster, than the inner one. The *differential* enables this to happen whilst both wheels are still being driven; it is housed within the final drive and consists of a further system of bevel gears. Of these, two, the differential gears, drive the axle shafts whilst the differential pinions mesh with them as shown. When the car is moving in a straight line both axles

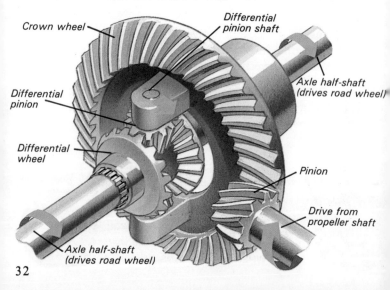

Crown wheel

Differential pinion shaft

Axle half-shaft (drives road wheel)

Differential pinion

Differential wheel

Pinion

Drive from propeller shaft

Axle half-shaft (drives road wheel)

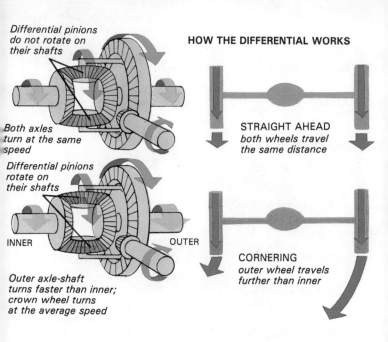

Differential pinions do not rotate on their shafts

Both axles turn at the same speed

HOW THE DIFFERENTIAL WORKS

STRAIGHT AHEAD *both wheels travel the same distance*

Differential pinions rotate on their shafts

INNER   OUTER

Outer axle-shaft turns faster than inner; crown wheel turns at the average speed

CORNERING *outer wheel travels further than inner*

rotate at the same speed and the differential pinions do not rotate on their shafts. However, when the car is cornering the axle shafts run at different speeds and the differential pinions rotate about their own axes to accommodate the difference.

Even though the differential gears are running at different speeds, the driving force is the same at each roadwheel. This can be a nuisance under slippery conditions because if one wheel slips then the other cannot develop sufficient force to get the car moving. Some expensive cars have 'limited slip' differentials to prevent this happening whilst tractors and many 'off-the-road' vehicles have 'locks' to cut out the differential action.

Overdrive

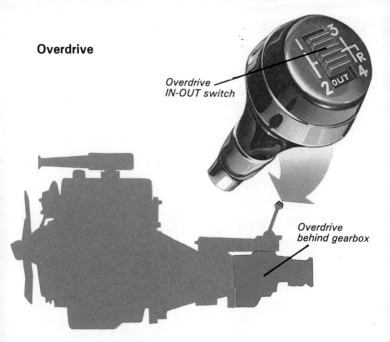

Overdrive
IN-OUT switch

Overdrive
behind gearbox

When cruising at steady high speeds it is found that many cars, especially the more powerful ones, can develop sufficient power with the engine running slower than it would normally do in top gear. Because of this, modern cars are being increasingly provided with a fifth gear whose gearbox ratio is such that the output shaft from the gearbox runs *faster* than the engine. This enables the car to cruise more quietly whilst at the same time using less fuel and causing less wear on the engine.

Another way of doing this is to fit an overdrive unit which is an auxiliary gearbox mounted behind the main one. This can be cut in or out electrically by means of a switch that is usually mounted on the gear lever. The overdrive can normally be operated when either top or third gears are engaged.

Automatic transmissions

Driving in towns where there is heavy traffic can be very tedious, requiring much gear-changing and use of the clutch. Many drivers prefer to have an automatic transmission so that they only need to press two pedals; the accelerator to make the car go and the brake pedal to stop it.

There are various types of automatic transmission but by far the most common employs a *torque converter* in front of an *epicyclic* gearbox.

A torque converter uses oil to transmit the drive from the engine to the gearbox. It can act as a clutch by taking up the drive smoothly when the car moves off; it can also act like a gearbox, multiplying the torque output (or turning effort) from the engine before passing it to the gearbox proper, albeit at a reduced speed.

Finally, at higher engine speeds the torque converter acts as a coupling, driving the gearbox with very little slip.

Because there is a torque converter, the gearbox of an automatic transmission does not need so many ratios; it usually has three. 'Epicyclic' gears are used because gear changes can be made with 'power on' and there is no need to de-clutch.

The automatic control system decides when the gear change is to be made by sensing both the vehicle's speed and the throttle opening. If the driver wants extra acceleration, say for overtaking, he can make the gearbox change to a lower gear, by temporarily pressing the accelerator to the floorboard; this is known as *kick down*.

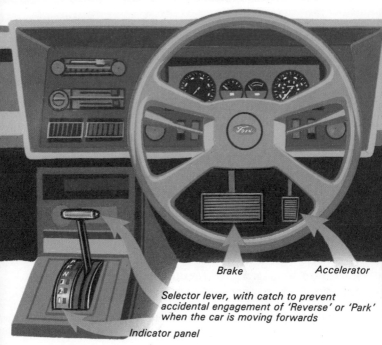

Brake Accelerator

Selector lever, with catch to prevent accidental engagement of 'Reverse' or 'Park' when the car is moving forwards

Indicator panel

The engine will only start with the selector lever at 'N' or 'P'

The diagram shows the driver's controls on a car with automatic transmission. P is the parked position when the transmission is locked and the vehicle cannot move; R is reverse; N is neutral with no gear engaged; D is the normal driving position with automatic gear changing in all the forward gears, whilst in 2 and 1 the transmission is prevented from changing to higher ratios.

Automatic transmissions, because of slip at the torque converter, tend to use more fuel than manual ones. In future we are likely to see transmissions where the gear ratios are infinitely variable and these ratios, together with engine throttle openings, are controlled by micro-processors.

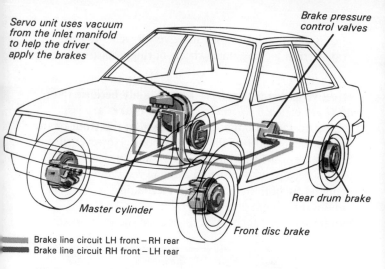

Servo unit uses vacuum from the inlet manifold to help the driver apply the brakes

Brake pressure control valves

Master cylinder

Rear drum brake

Front disc brake

Brake line circuit LH front – RH rear
Brake line circuit RH front – LH rear

The braking system

Braking force comes from friction between the tyre and the road and this in turn depends upon the load on the tyre. When a car is stopping, load is transferred from the rear wheels to the front and so front brakes are designed to do about seventy per cent of the work.

The diagram above shows a typical braking system of a modern car. It has disc brakes at the front and drum brakes at the rear. When the driver pushes the brake pedal, a piston in the master cylinder displaces hydraulic fluid in the brake pipes which in turn pushes on the pistons in the wheel cylinders and so causes them to operate the brakes.

Typically, on a modern front wheel drive car, there are two hydraulic systems, each connected to a front and a rear wheel. This is known as a 'diagonal split' and ensures that should there be a leak in either system at least a half of the braking force will still be available.

The 'Brake Pressure Control Valve' prevents the rear brakes from locking their wheels during a hard stop.

When a brake gets very hot it is liable to become less effective and is then said to *fade*. Mainly because the discs are exposed to cooling air, disc brakes are less subject to fade and are therefore used at the front of the vehicle where most of the work is done. However, drum brakes are still fitted almost universally to the rear wheels because it is easier to arrange for them to be actuated by both hydraulic and mechanical means. A handbrake system is required by law and so the handbrake is arranged also to operate the rear brakes.

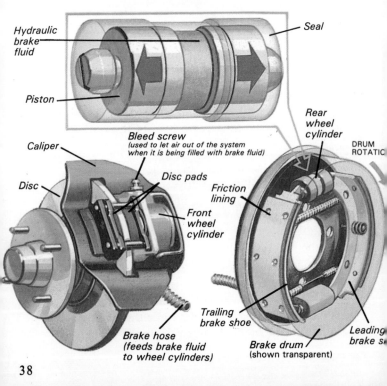

Hydraulic brake fluid

Seal

Piston

Rear wheel cylinder

DRUM ROTATIO

Caliper

Bleed screw
(used to let air out of the system
when it is being filled with brake fluid)

Disc pads

Friction lining

Disc

Front wheel cylinder

Trailing brake shoe

Brake hose
(feeds brake fluid
to wheel cylinders)

Brake drum
(shown transparent)

Leading
brake s

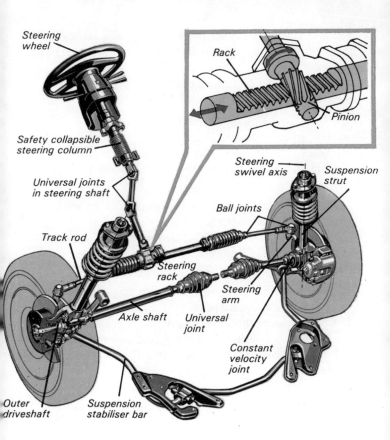

Steering

All cars steer by turning the front wheels and nearly all modern cars do this by means of a *rack and pinion* as in the diagram above. You will see that the pinion is a small gear which is turned by the steering wheel via the steering shaft. The rack is a flat set of gear teeth which is moved to and fro by the pinion, pushing one track rod and pulling the other, thus turning both wheels in the same direction about their respective swivel axes. The track rods have ball joints at each end to allow the wheels to move up and down with the springing; these have to be carefully positioned so that the wheel movement does not affect the steering.

The suspension struts that support the car at the front are free to turn because there are bearings at the top and bottom and so these form the swivel axes for the front wheels.

These axes are not quite perpendicular to the road but lean inwards and backwards slightly at the top. This helps to make the steering lighter and produces castor action (as in a tea trolley) to straighten the wheels when coming out of a corner.

There are universal joints in the steering shaft and the steering column is collapsible; these are safety features. If in an accident the front suspension is pushed backwards, the steering shaft will fold and the steering column will not be pushed back into the passenger compartment.

Also, if the driver is thrown forward on to the steering wheel the steering column will collapse and absorb the impact; in addition the steering wheel is itself flat and yielding to prevent damage to the driver's chest.

Refer now to the diagram opposite. Since the rear wheels do not steer, the car turns about a point along the line of the rear axle as at (b). It follows that the inner front wheel must turn through a greater angle than the outer one. This can be achieved approximately by arranging for the steering arms to point inwards. Their lines of centres meet at a distance of about two-thirds of the wheelbase from the front axle. This is known as the *Ackerman Principle*.

It is now known however that for a tyre to develop a sideways force for cornering it has to point at a slight angle inwards ('slip angle') from the direction in which it is moving. This means that under hard cornering, the front wheels should turn through nearly equal angles, making them almost parallel to one another. In practice the designer compromises so that the relationship between the steered angles of the two front wheels lies between parallel and that required by the Ackerman principle.

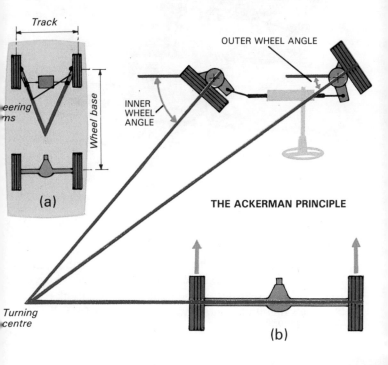

Track

eering
ms

Wheel base

(a)

OUTER WHEEL ANGLE

INNER
WHEEL
ANGLE

THE ACKERMAN PRINCIPLE

Turning
centre

(b)

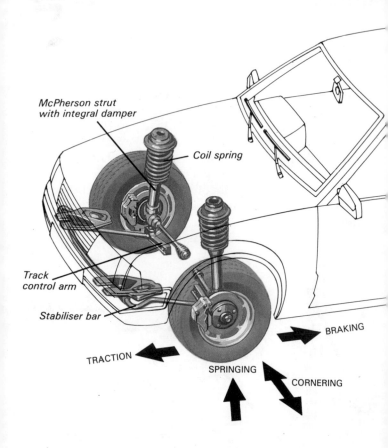

McPherson strut with integral damper

Coil spring

Track control arm

Stabiliser bar

TRACTION

BRAKING

SPRINGING

CORNERING

Suspension

A vehicle's suspension has to perform three important functions. First it has to isolate the driver and passengers from road irregularities; secondly it has to ensure that the wheels maintain contact with the road; and thirdly, it must be so designed that the vehicle handles in a satisfactory manner.

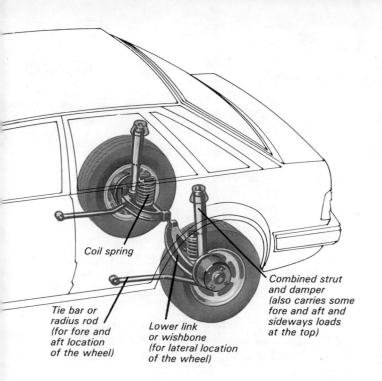

Coil spring

Combined strut
and damper
(also carries some
fore and aft and
sideways loads
at the top)

Tie bar or
radius rod
(for fore and
aft location
of the wheel)

Lower link
or wishbone
(for lateral location
of the wheel)

The vehicle illustrated above has modern coil spring
suspension at both ends. At the front the coil springs are
more or less directly over the wheels but at the rear the
springs have to work against a leverage.

You will see that the stabiliser bar goes across the
front of the car and is part of the suspension at both
sides. When both wheels strike a bump the bar just
rotates in its mountings but if one wheel goes up and the
other down then the stabiliser bar twists and offers
resistance, so trying to prevent the roll of the body. For
this reason the stabiliser bar is sometimes called an 'anti-
roll bar'.

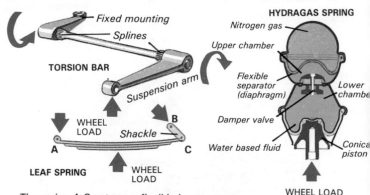

TORSION BAR

Fixed mounting
Splines
Suspension arm

HYDRAGAS SPRING

Nitrogen gas
Upper chamber
Flexible separator (diaphragm)
Lower chamber
Damper valve
Water based fluid
Conical piston

WHEEL LOAD

LEAF SPRING

WHEEL LOAD
Shackle
A
B
C
WHEEL LOAD

The spring A C acts as a flexible beam which bends under the action of the wheel load

When a wheel strikes a bump the spring deflects, allowing the wheel to move upwards whilst the body of the vehicle remains more or less level. If it were left to its own devices, the body would bounce on the spring. To prevent this, dampers are fitted between the wheels and the body. The dampers are often referred to as 'shock absorbers' but this is not strictly true. The road spring absorbs the shock and the damper controls the ensuing vibration.

The wheel, brakes and associated parts can move between the road spring and the tyre, which is itself a sort of stiff spring; this system will also have its own natural frequency. When the wheel is rotating at speed it will tend to develop *wheel hop*, especially if the wheel is out of balance or out of round. This should be controlled by the dampers but can frequently be seen on cars on the motorway travelling at 105–120 km/h (65–75 mph).

There are, of course, many kinds of springs used on motor cars and three of these are shown above. The torsion bar relies upon the twisting of a metal bar to provide a springing action; a coil spring is really a torsion bar that has been wrapped into a helix. The leaf spring consists of a number of metal plates which together constitute a flexible beam that bends to provide the springing action. Note that the spring is attached to the vehicle at A and B through the shackle BC. The shackle can rotate about B and is necessary to accommodate the change in length of AC when the spring changes shape.

The *hydragas* spring depends upon the compression of nitrogen gas and upon the change in effective area of the conical piston as it moves upward to produce both an increasing load and an increasing spring stiffness. This results in the very desirable characteristic for a road-spring of increasing stiffnesses with wheel deflection.

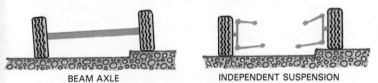

BEAM AXLE   INDEPENDENT SUSPENSION

The car on pages 42 and 43 has independent strut suspension on all four wheels – this means that each wheel is independently attached to the vehicle structure. Another popular form of independent suspension is shown above. It will be seen that if one wheel goes over a bump the wheel at the other side is more or less unaffected. Important advantages are that more of the car's weight is supported by the road springs and that the car can have a soft suspension without its rolling excessively on a corner. There are, however, disadvantages. Most benefits accrue from fitting independent suspension at the front and some cars continue to be fitted with the simpler non-independent suspensions at the rear.

Alternator, battery and starter

The electric power used throughout the car is provided by the alternator which is driven from the engine by a vee-belt and pulleys. However, the alternator cannot produce power when the engine is not running and so energy is stored in the battery as chemical energy.

The alternator has now superseded the dynamo because of its reliability and higher output, especially at low speeds; this makes it especially suitable for modern vehicles which have high electrical loading.

The battery contains diluted sulphuric acid which is called the *electrolyte*; this must always be above the level of the lead plates that are contained within the battery. When necessary, the battery is topped up with distilled or de-ionised water but the trend now is for batteries that are 'sealed for life' and need no topping up. All batteries used on modern cars are now 12 volt.

The starter takes an extremely high current (250–500 amps) but fortunately only for a short time. This current is too high to pass through the ignition/starter switch which instead operates a solenoid switch in the engine compartment. The solenoid closes the contacts of a heavy duty switch connecting specially thick cables from the battery to the starter motor.

The starter is a *Direct Current* series wound motor that provides a high turning effort at low speeds. The pinion is mounted on a threaded sleeve on the shaft of the starter. When the starter is switched on, the pinion moves along the shaft to engage a geared ring on the engine's flywheel, and this rotates the engine to start it. When the engine starts, the pinion is thrown back along the thread and out of engagement.

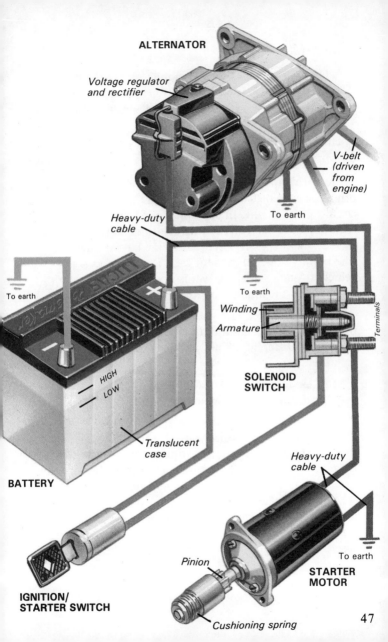

ALTERNATOR

Voltage regulator and rectifier

V-belt (driven from engine)

To earth

Heavy-duty cable

To earth

To earth

Winding

Armature

Terminals

SOLENOID SWITCH

−

+

HIGH

LOW

Translucent case

BATTERY

Heavy-duty cable

To earth

Pinion

STARTER MOTOR

Cushioning spring

IGNITION/ STARTER SWITCH

47

The electrical system

A motor car could not run without an electrical system. Electricity is needed to turn the engine, operate the ignition and power the lights, instruments and accessories.

The battery is used to store the electrical energy for use when the engine is not running.

Electrical equipment requires two connections: one to bring the current from the battery and the other to complete the circuit. In cars, only one lead is used for each circuit as the current returns to the battery through the body and chassis. One lead of the battery therefore (the negative one on modern cars) is *earthed* to the vehicle structure. This system is known as *earth return* and reduces the amount of wiring by half.

For convenience, wires that lead to adjacent areas of the car are bound together into a 'loom'. Individual wires have different colour markings so that they can be identified.

Most circuits are protected by fuses. This saves damage to the vehicle's wiring and electrical components and avoids the risk of fire.

In the diagram opposite you will find that circuits (e g, the lights) that are connected to fuse 1 are fed directly from the battery but that those connected to fuse 2 (such as the horn, indicators, brake lights, windscreen wipers etc.) are controlled by the ignition switch and will therefore not operate when the engine is switched off. The ignition circuit itself is not usually protected by a fuse. In practice there are many more fuses than shown.

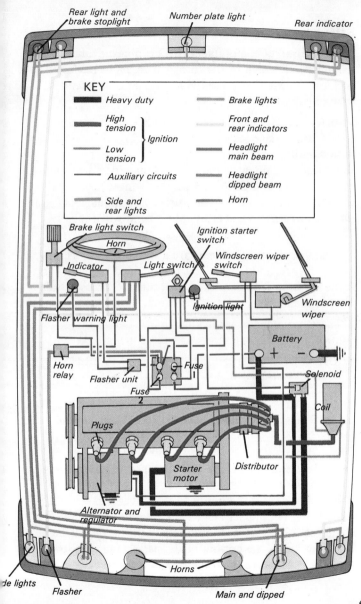

Rear light and brake stoplight

Number plate light

Rear indicator

KEY

Heavy duty		Brake lights
High tension	} Ignition	Front and rear indicators
Low tension		Headlight main beam
Auxiliary circuits		Headlight dipped beam
Side and rear lights		Horn

Brake light switch

Horn

Ignition starter switch

Windscreen wiper switch

Indicator

Light switch

Flasher warning light

Ignition light

Windscreen wiper

Battery

Horn relay

Flasher unit

Fuse 1

Solenoid

Fuse 2

Coil

Plugs

Distributor

Starter motor

Alternator and regulator

de lights

Flasher

Horns

Main and dipped

49

Safety

Vehicle safety comes under two headings; primary and secondary. The aim of the former is to avoid having accidents in the first place, whilst the latter is intended to avoid or minimise injury.

Primary Safety The vehicle should have good handling with a progressive response to the steering. When the limit of adhesion is reached during cornering, the car should not break-away and spin but should rather come out of a bend at a tangent, with the front wheels tending to go straight on. Front wheel drive cars should not *tuck-in* or turn more sharply into a bend when the driver's foot is lifted off the accelerator.

Dual circuit brake systems are also important, as are plastic coated brake pipes that are shielded by bodywork from abrasion from stones or exposure to corrosive salt off the roads in the winter.

There are many other features in car design that contribute to primary safety and these include:

GOOD ACCELERATION – ALL ROUND VISIBILITY – CONTROLS AND ADEQUATE INSTRUMENTS IN THE CORRECT POSITION – GOOD HEATING AND VENTILATION, COMFORTABLE SEATING – WARNING LIGHTS – *e g, brake lining wear, fluid level, seat belts not worn.* – GOOD LIGHTING AND VISIBILITY – *the driver should have adequate vision at night and the car be easily seen.*

Secondary Safety Cars are now designed to have crumple zones at the front and rear. These absorb the shock of impact and reduce the injury to the driver and passengers. On impact neither the steering wheel nor the engine should be forced into the passenger compartment. The diagram at the bottom of the page opposite shows some safety features incorporated in modern cars.

CRUMPLE ZONES

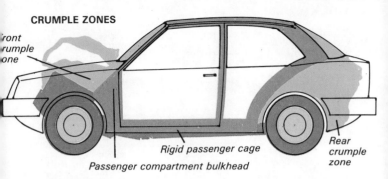

Front crumple zone

Rear crumple zone

Rigid passenger cage

Passenger compartment bulkhead

DIAGRAM OF SAFETY FEATURES

1   Low front end – bonnet line so that if a pedestrian should be struck he will go over the bonnet rather than under the car

2   Laminated windscreen

3   Reinforcing beam across middle of door to resist side impact

4   No interior or exterior sharp corners

5   Motorway rear red lights

6   Fuel tank away from the rear of the car

7   Seat belt and anchorage

8   Anti-burst door locks

9   Warning lights on instrument panel

10 Padded steering wheel with broad spokes and energy absorbing collapsible column and universal joint

11 Head restraints – to prevent whip lash of the neck if the car is struck from behind

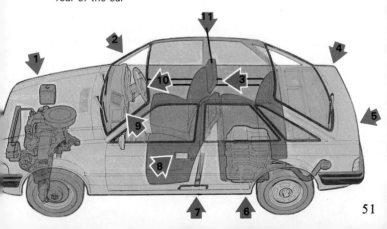

INDEX